This book belongs to

Wyatt Haser

This is dedicated to my husband, Matthew,
whose support made my dream a reality,
and to Ian and Madeleine,
my little sunshine and moonbeam.

Copyright © 2017 Alayna Gagnier

ISBN-13: 978-1548161064

ISBN-10: 1548161063

Illustrations Copyright © 2017 Alayna Gagnier

Goat Bought a Boat

By Alayna Gagnier
Illustrated by Jessica Gibson

Goat bought a boat
He thought it would float
And take his friends out to sea

Engine goes ...

Sinking swiftly
down
down
down

"We all drink water," Horse starts to say.
"Let's grab straws and drink the sea away!"

Pig taps his head and snorts with delight.
"I have an idea that might be alright!

We've got hooves, powerful and strong.
Let's kick the water out. That can't take long!"

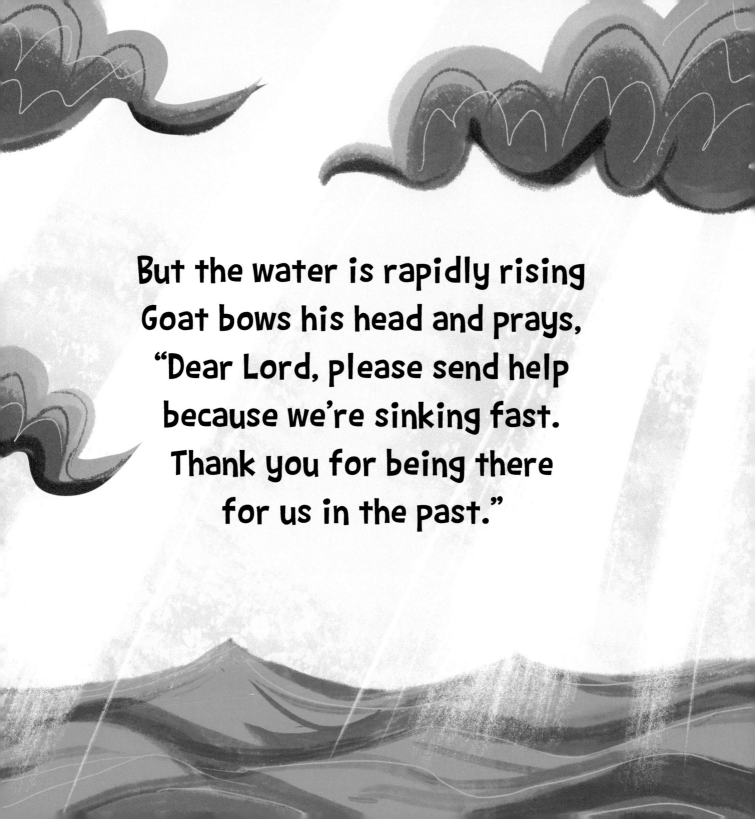

But the water is rapidly rising
Goat bows his head and prays,
"Dear Lord, please send help
because we're sinking fast.
Thank you for being there
for us in the past."

Goat opens his eyes and what should appear
Water spouting and a black dorsal fin
drawing near

Orca smiles, "Jump on board if you
want a ride."
Quickly they climb onto Orca's top side

Orca jumps up. Orca dives down.
Orca is the coolest ride in town

On shore they're safe at last
Cheering as they step onto the grass

At home Goat stops to think,
"I'm so lucky to have a God who cares,
Who promises to always be there.
No matter if I'm on land or at sea
With me always that's where God will be."

With that thought he drifts
slowly slowly slowly off to sleep.

Alayna Gagnier lives with her husband, their two adorable children, Ian and Madeleine, and their beloved dog, Keanu, in the great Pacific Northwest.

Made in the USA
Lexington, KY
16 September 2017